WITHDRAWN

LLAMA DESTROYS THE WORLD

I am Llama.

JONATHAN STUTZMAN

Illustrated by HEATHER FOX

Henry Holt and Company ✦ New York

Henry Holt and Company, *Publishers since 1866*
Henry Holt® is a registered trademark of Macmillan Publishing Group, LLC
175 Fifth Avenue, New York, NY 10010
mackids.com

Library of Congress Cataloging-in-Publication Data
Names: Stutzman, Jonathan, author. | Fox, Heather, illustrator.
Title: Llama destroys the world / Jonathan Stutzman ; illustrated by Heather Fox.
Description: First edition. | New York : Henry Holt and Company, 2019. |
Summary: Eating too much cake causes Llama to rip his dancing pants,
opening a black hole and threatening the entire universe.
Identifiers: LCCN 2018038285 | ISBN 9781250303172 (hardcover)
Subjects: | CYAC: Llamas—Fiction. | Black holes (Astronomy)—Fiction. |
Humorous stories.
Classification: LCC PZ7.1.S798 Ll 2019 | DDC [E]—dc23
LC record available at https://lccn.loc.gov/2018038285

Our books may be purchased in bulk for promotional, educational, or business use.
Please contact your local bookseller or the Macmillan Corporate and Premium Sales Department
at (800) 221-7945 ext. 5442 or by email at MacmillanSpecialMarkets@macmillan.com.

First edition, 2019 / Designed by April Ward
The illustrations for this book were created digitally.
Printed in China by RR Donnelley Asia Printing Solutions Ltd., Dongguan City, Guangdong Province
1 3 5 7 9 10 8 6 4 2

To Christian and Elena,

for helping us destroy the world

On Friday, Llama will destroy the world.

proclaimed
Llama.

MONDAY

On Monday, Llama found cake.

Piles of cake. More cake than any llama should ever eat.

"dat" said Llama.

Llama ate all of the cake.

This was his first mistake.

It was an honest mistake.
It was a delicious mistake.
One of those mistakes that
leads to more mistakes and,
eventually, the ultimate
doom of everything.

TUESDAY

Tuesdays were for dancing,
so Llama put on his dancing pants.

The pants did not fit.
(He was still full of cake.)

But he never danced without
his dancing pants; they made
his butt look groovy.

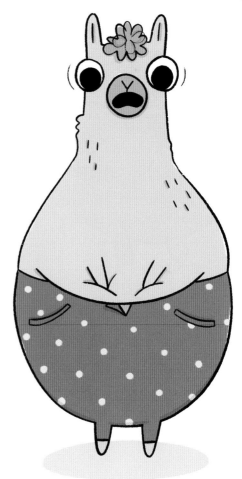

So Llama huffed and puffed . . .

. . . and squeezed and stuffed
himself into the pants.
This was his second mistake.

And then Llama danced.

He jigged.

He tangoed.

He cha-cha'ed real smooth.

His rhythm was perfect, his moves were precise...but the pants never stood a chance.

The rip was thunderous. It shook the house, the trees, and the mountains. It shook the very fabric of the universe.

The cosmic vibrations from the ripping pants were so mighty that a black hole tore open.

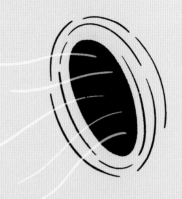

WEDNESDAY

On Wednesday, Llama found the black hole.

"dat" said Llama.

He had never seen a black hole before. He didn't know what it could be . . . or what it could do. But Llama was a llama of science. He knew the answers were out there, waiting to be discovered.

Llama read books.

He ran complex experiments.

He debated with the greatest minds and thinkers he could find.

And then he analyzed the data and came to a well-thought-out conclusion.

dat

said Llama wisely.

Instead of warning the world of its imminent doom, Llama decided to do something more important . . . he made a bologna and cheese sandwich, with extra cheese.

This was his third mistake.

THURSDAY

On Thursday, many signs of doom
appeared in the sky.

Flying top hats. Soaring teacups. Twisting, tumbling, well-dressed turtles. But Llama didn't notice.

Thursdays were for painting, and Llama was busy painting his latest masterpiece.

The end was near.

On Friday, the world ended. The more the black hole sucked in, the bigger and stronger it grew.

The animals flew.
The pizzas and bicycles
and houseplants flew.
And Llama flew, too.

The black hole swallowed everything up. Every single thing left in the world. Everything left in the *universe*.

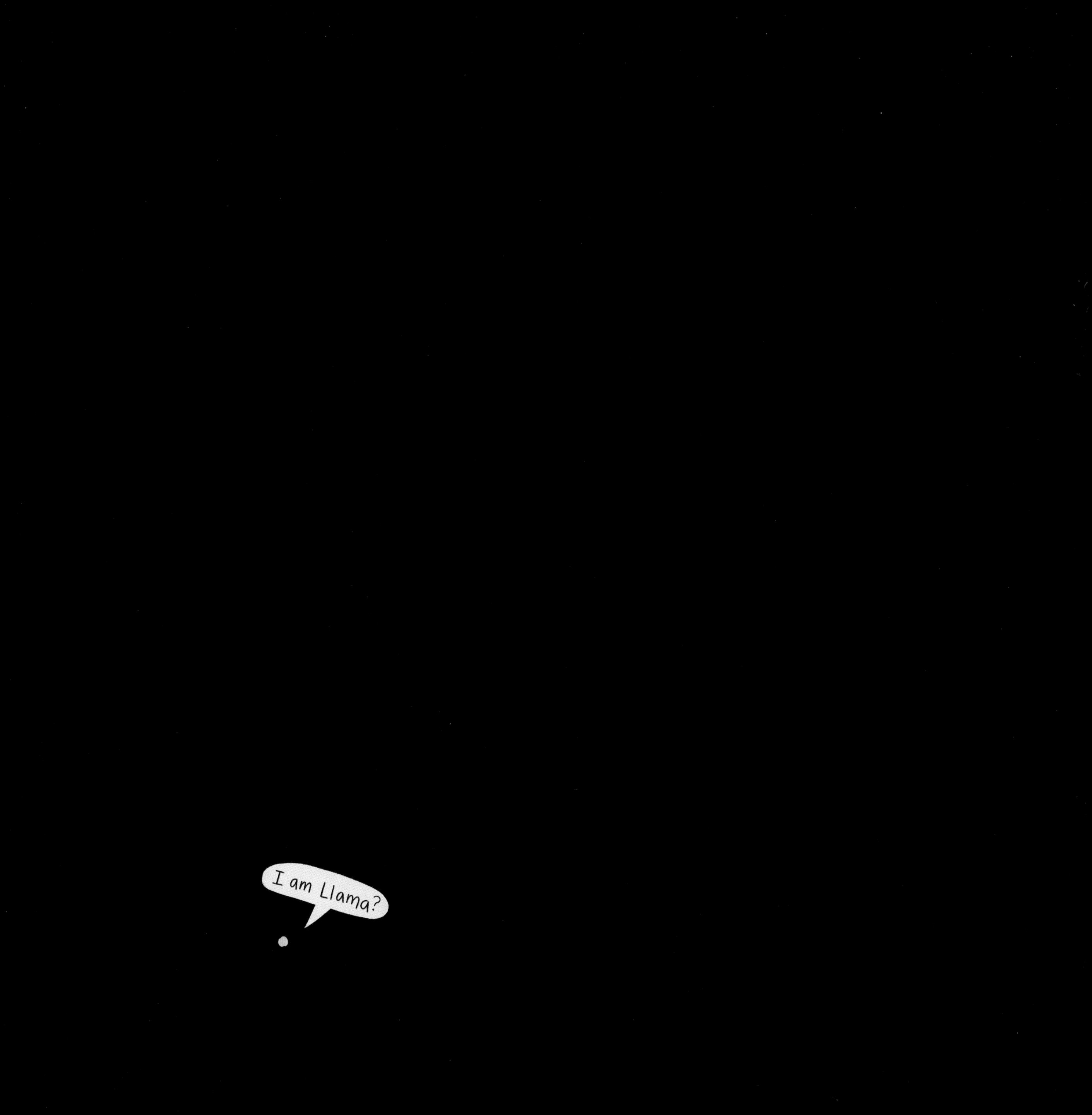
I am Llama?

Until there was nothing.

SATURDAY

On Saturday, on the other side
of the black hole, everything was fine.

The universe tumbled out exactly as it had been before. Even Llama.

I am Llama!

proclaimed Llama.

The sky was blue. The sun was shining.
The world was perfectly calm,
like nothing had ever happened.

SUNDAY

On Sunday, with the world back to normal . . .
Llama found something wonderful.

Piles of pie.

More pie than any llama should ever eat.

"dat" said Llama.

Llama ate all of the pie.